GW01417609

Madness in March

by
Sheena Chisnell

Bloomington, IN   Milton Keynes, UK

authorHOUSE®

AuthorHouse™
1663 Liberty Drive, Suite 200
Bloomington, IN 47403
www.authorhouse.com
Phone: 1-800-839-8640

AuthorHouse™ UK Ltd.
500 Avebury Boulevard
Central Milton Keynes, MK9 2BE
www.authorhouse.co.uk
Phone: 08001974150

First published by AuthorHouse 1/8/2007

ISBN: 978-1-4259-7502-9 (sc)

Printed in the United States of America
Bloomington, Indiana

This book is printed on acid-free paper.

Madness in March

—◆—

To:- Kath
Mary   Blessings

Sheena J. Chesnell

3rd March 2007

Prologue 1951

She was standing at the highest point on the island, known as Bix Top Face gazing out towards the Atlantic Ocean. Today the sea seemed to her to be misbehaving, the white waves appeared terrifyingly high as they crashed with such a din on the rocks below with white foam cascading like a waterfall.

Belle was all of ten years old today 1st March 1951 and she was fed up. Mum had said, today she would have her hair cut, just as she had every year previous, as far back as she could remember on her birthday. Belle thought, how I can ever become a film star if Mum keeps cutting my hair.

Mum, Dad and the sisters and brothers of both families had this thing about Lent. It didn't make any difference when Lent started, even if it was in February, the McCullum and the McDonald family on the 1st March suffered from this Madness of all the females having there hair cut and attending the Kirk every day until the end of the month.

Belle would ask why this madness existed in our family but Mum would just mumble 'it is a McCullum and a McDonald tradition.' As she stood watching the rollers come in and wash over the rocks she heard the voices of her sisters, Lily and Marie. They were older than Belle by three and four years respectively, and thought they were rather grown up.

Belle heard part of what they were saying.

'I am not having my hair cut' Lily was saying to Marie,

'And neither am I,' said Marie.

They suddenly saw Belle and shouted,

'C'mon Belle, we're off to Maisie's.'

Belle was wondering why her sisters were so friendly. Usually they moaned if she had to go with them, particularly when they were walking to and from school.

As sisters they were very unalike. Marie at fourteen was blue-eyed, short and plump with blonde curly hair that she detested. She was a real bossy boots and quite spiteful at times, particularly with Belle. Lily at thirteen was tall, slim with flashing deep violet eyes, her hair being a deeper blonde than Marie's. She was aware that she was attractive; the boys were always hanging around her.

Belle, the youngest was quite tall for her age with thick wavy hair described as a brunette with deep brown expressive eyes. She was a dreamy child and never seemed to feel that she belonged to her family. Belle knew she was different, well, that is what her Mum said when she was born, a throw back to previous generations.

All three girls were now moaning about the hair cutting ceremony that Mum would perform at 2.00pm. She didn't have any idea on hairdressing, just took the scissors and cut their hair in line with their ears.

The girls agreed that they would stick together and let her know that their hair would not be cut this year whether it was tradition or not. They were not joining in this March Madness. Thus in the intermittent sunshine they climbed the long steep hill to their friend Maisie's family cottage and together they hatched their plans, whereby they would arrive home at about 4.00pm. Mum would be in the dairy helping Dad with the milking. There would be no time to cut hair before tea. Then they had to go to the Kirk for another boring hour. By the time they arrived home it would be bedtime. Maisie suggested to the three sisters they find the scissors and bury them in the field on the farm.

On the way home bossy Marie as usual took charge and told Belle,

'You find the scissors Belle; you Lily dig a little hole in the field at the back of the house and put the scissors there. Cover the patch up with some of the leaves lying around along with some stones. I will watch out for Duncan and Dougie and divert their attention.'

The boys, identical twins of seven years made up the rest of the family. They resembled Marie and Lily and were always playing tricks on their Mum, Dad and sisters. Mum would say 'c'mon Duncan get ready for school,' and he would say 'I'm Dougie'. This happened time and time again at home and school until the teacher decided to mark the back of their necks with different coloured ink. It was a real laugh at times.

Chapter 1

-March 1961-

Belle stood again at the cliff top of Bix Top Face. The sun was high in the heavens, it was midday and large billowy white clouds seemed to be suspended from a beautiful light blue sky. The promise of spring and summer had finally arrived. Belle gazed out on the Atlantic Ocean recalling ten years ago the plans to stop the March Madness that pervaded her family. When they had hatched their plans to hide the scissors, Mum was furious, but it had been the last year of hair cutting. With a smile on her face she retraced her steps towards the farm, which looked warm and comforting, thinking what a lot has happened in these intervening years.

The twins, Duncan and Dougie now seventeen, still playing tricks on Mum. Both were studying to take their Highers. Duncan had great ambitions of being a vet and Dougie equally ambitious had an inkling to do research medicine. They had dreams of making pots of money in their chosen careers and travelling all over the world. For now they were living on mainland with Uncle Jimmy, Mum's brother, and his family so that they could attend College

Bossy boots Marie at 24 still lived at home, with her baby, Andrew of eighteen months. Who would have believed it, Marie with a baby? Belle mused I would love to know who is Andrew's father. Marie always right, always argumentative, always better than anyone else had come unstuck. According to Mum's letters Dad wanted to throw her out when she became pregnant, especially as Marie would not divulge who the father was, but Mum insisted that she be at home.

Another thing about family tradition was that unless Marie agreed to be churched she and Andrew would be cast out of the local society. Her Mother had told her that she had to go to the Kirk to ask God for forgiveness for her sins, namely having Andrew out of wedlock. Normally, after having a baby you went to the Kirk to offer thanksgiving for a safe birth. In the end Marie had given in not for her sake, 'cause she didn't believe in all that rubbish, but for her son's future. Andrew still had not been baptized and this was a source of pain to Mum as folks kept asking,

'When's the bairn going to be done?'

Mum was so scared of what people would say or what they might do to Marie, her favourite daughter. Despite Marie's shame Belle felt a little guilty that she couldn't love her sister like the others in her family.

Lily at 23 had just qualified as a Staff Nurse at Edinburgh Royal Infirmary. She too was coming home on a week's holiday and was so excited as she told her Mum and Dad that she had met a young man called Craig. According to Lily he had been a patient on the ward where she was nursing and they had fallen in love. He was obviously the bee's knees. Mum and Dad kept their counsel.

Yes, a lot had happened in ten years. Going to Kirk every day during Lent was still very much part of the family life and those who lived in the small community of Riarch. Belle believed that it was a ritual performed out of fear rather than love. She bounced down towards the farmhouse, being greeted by Bess and Tess Dad's seven-month-old boisterous Border Collies pups. They were being trained to herd the sheep, but at present they were just playful. She was looking forward to hearing all the Riarch gossip. As she opened the back door there was an almighty argument going on between Mum and Dad. Mum was accusing Dad of having an affair with "that blowsy hussy half his age, at number sixteen in the village". Dad's face went purple with rage. Belle had never seen her Dad in such a rage. He retorted,

'You dare to say that to me after what you did. All these years we've been wed, never a word as to the father of our Belle. Yes, Hannah, your secret is out, I

4

know that Belle is not mine, but I love her as my own child, aye more than you know, so you can't talk'

As they both turned, Belle was standing at the back door. Mum looked embarrassed and whispered,

'Belle, why didn't you let us know that you were coming home today'? Belle felt her whole world collapse, although she had sometimes felt like an outsider in the family, she nevertheless idolized her Dad.

' I thought I would give you a surprise and now I wish I hadn't walked over the threshold. Mum what is happening, why are you saying those things about Dad?'

With tears streaming down her face Belle then said,

'What do you mean Dad? Am I not your daughter?'

Mum just looked deflated and all of a sudden Belle thought she looked ill. Belle flew upstairs to the bedroom she had occupied with her sisters when they were all children, threw herself on the bed, the tears welling up wracking her body with pain. She had always known she was different to her brothers and sisters but had pushed these thoughts to the back of her mind over the years. Now everything was collapsing around her and the questions crowding her mind, who was she? Who was her father? She felt sick as she could still hear Mum's words in her mind,

'Our Belle is a throwback to previous generations'

She fell asleep weary with crying.

Chapter 2

When Belle awoke she thought that she had had a nightmare, and then soon realized that this was no flipping nightmare. It was a hell, present and real. The family she loved was no more. How could Mum and Dad betray each other and above all lie to her? She felt a hot rage coursing through her body. How could her Mum do this to her? Belle felt her stomach churning. She almost threw up in her panic. Should she return to Newcastle, to the security of the family who employed her as a Nanny to their three children?

As all these thoughts crowded her mind, Marie walked in with her son, sat down on the bed, and put her arms round Belle, saying,

'Don't take on Sis; it's not the end of the world.'

'What do you mean, not the end of the world, anyway what do you know' said Belle through her angry tears,

'Did you know that I am not your sister?'

Marie looked shocked, noticing Belle's red puffy eyes.

'What do you mean; of course you are my sister.'

'No. I am not,' screamed Belle. I walked in when Mum and Dad were rowing, Mum accusing Dad of having an affair and he shouted, 'I know that Belle is not mine.'

Marie didn't quite know what to say to this, so she gathered Andrew into her arms and said to Belle.

'Let's go downstairs and ask Mum and Dad to tell us the truth, after all we are not children anymore.'

Before they opened the bedroom door, Mum came in crying and looked as if she were about to collapse. At that moment in time Belle hated her mother remembering the words

'Our Belle's a throwback to previous generations.'

Mum couldn't bring herself to face her daughters; she just sat down on the bed cradling Andrew who had tottered over to his Gran as she came into room. Hannah longed to take Belle in her arms and tell her the truth, but couldn't find her tongue. The pain she experienced was too strong. She knew in her heart that Belle would now reject her love. This was her secret which she had locked away for all those years. It was her secret that now was no longer and it threatened to split her beloved family.

Belle gave her mother a cold stare, screaming,

'I hate you, I hate you. I don't want you as my mother any more and I don't want to see you again. Do you hear what I am saying, I do not want to see you, ever.'

She grabbed her coat and ran downstairs, out of the home that she so loved, but now hated and made her way up to Bix Top Face. She wanted to be alone. She had only been home two hours. Belle started climbing down the cliff side to the hideaway cave, which as children they had spent hours in between tides. It was their secret hideaway. She did wonder if the stubs of candles and matches were still in the hole at top of the cave. Yes, they were still there after all those years. Belle along with her sisters had dreamt of their futures in this hideway. She thought that's all they were dreams.

Today the Atlantic Ocean was serene, very blue and gave off a feeling of peace, yet there was an uneasy calm, an atmosphere which Belle couldn't quite understand. The day also had a gloomy feel about it as if it was waiting for the worst to happen.

The seagulls usually screeching and dipping low were not to be seen. The grey seals normally cavorting on the rocks had disappeared, yet there was a watery sunshine filtering through the clouds. Belle felt the hot rage just slipping away and suddenly tiredness seemed to envelop her whole being, especially after her long train journey from Newcastle, then the Ferry Crossing. In the hideaway she felt safe and thought I'll just have a nap then decide what to do.

Meanwhile outside the weather suddenly changed from a quiet and calm day to one of sheer terror with thunder and lightening with the awful roar of the sea. It seemed that it had been whipped up in a giant mixer ready to spiral out of control. The wind was howling its way through the hideaway, making it feel eerie. Belle awoke with a start realizing something had changed. She looked out of the hideaway and saw to her horror huge rollers beginning to crash in towards her hideaway. The sky had darkened somewhat; a solitary flash of lightening followed by the ominous rumble of thunder was evidence that the gods Thor and Neptune were conspiring to make this a day to remember.

Belle was absolutely terrified, hadn't Dad warned them as children about going down the cliff face, hadn't he instilled in them how quickly the weather can change on these islands. Hadn't he told them to always watch over to the North? Poor Dad didn't even know that they used to go down the cliff to the caves. For a few seconds Belle was rooted to the wet floor of the hideaway, thinking I am going to die, I am going to die.

She thought she could hear a voice in the distance calling,

'Belle where are you…?'

No, it was all in her frightened imagination. The wind was howling its head off and making all sorts of weird sounds. Then she heard it again, 'Belle, Belle.' It sounded like Uncle Callum's voice. He was Dad's second younger brother. Belle shouted with all the strength she could muster,

'I am down here. Please help me; the sea is coming towards me. I am frightened, I am going to drown, please come quickly,

Uncle Callum shouted above the din of the thunder,

'I am coming down, start coming out, even if you have to swim.'

Belle now gingerly moved from the spot where she had just stood, when a big roller knocked her over, and she could feel herself being dragged down to the depths of the seabed. She started fighting and pushed herself upwards towards the surface, and seeing a jagged rock just a few yards ahead of her, she began to swim towards it. Belle had always been a strong swimmer but in these weather conditions, even the best of swimmers could still drown.

Uncle Callum could see his beloved niece struggling to stay afloat. He began to slide quickly down the cliff face, risking his own life, but he too knew the cliff face like the back of his hand. He found himself perilously perched on a rock and as he bent over he was within reaching distance of Belle. He called to her,

'Belle, Belle can you hear me?' But his words were lost in the howling wind and the uproar of the sea, the lashing rain and huge bangs of thunder and lightening. As he inched ever closer he had confidence that he could grab her from the swirling angry sea. With an almighty stretch hanging on to the rock with one hand he pulled Belle out of the raging, noisy sea. Uncle Callum was physically spent but he drew on deep reserves of will power and dragged an almost unconscious Belle up the cliff face a little at a time.

Her legs were bleeding from the sharp stony face but he had to keep going. By now the whole family was out looking for Belle, and Callum could hear them coming closer.

'Thank God he muttered, Thank God. Why ever lass were you doing down the cliff face?'

In the biting howling wind, accompanied with horizontal rain Dad and Callum carried Belle to the farmhouse. Dad was shouting to Hannah and girls

'Get a move on, otherwise we will all be lost in this storm.'

After struggling with the dead weight of Belle and Uncle Callum nearing collapse they finally reached the farm.

Mum, with a ghost-like face just stood and wept inconsolably whilst Dad just shouted! 'Blast you woman, go and get some blankets and see to our Belle's needs. It's all our fault, God forgive us.'

Uncle Callum was slumped in the chair, exhausted and feeling a bit non-plussed as to what had happened and his brother's frenzied word 'it's all our fault', but he kept these thoughts to himself. Hannah didn't even look at Callum which he thought a bit strange, as usually she was always more than pleased to see him. Their only concern had to be Belle..

Chapter 3

$\mathcal{W}$hen Belle awoke the next morning, the sudden frightening storm had evaporated and shafts of bright sunlight were streaming through the bedroom window. She relived the horrors of the past few hours, thinking again it was indeed a terrible dream. Marie was lying on the bed just holding and cradling her like she would her own son Andrew. Marie who had always scoffed and ignored her younger sister was now the strong and caring one. Belle soon realized what was happening to her was real and, although fortunate that Uncle Callum had been there at the right time her, she wished he had left her to the sea.

Marie told her that when the weather changed Dad had said that he was going out to look for Belle. On the way towards Bix Top Face he called in at his brother's cottage and had asked Uncle Callum to come with him to find Belle. So the brothers set out and Callum instinctively seemed to know where Belle would be, but suggested to her Dad that he climb the hill to Maisie's cottage and he himself would go to Bix Top Face.

As Marie was relating all this to Belle, the bedroom door opened and Mum stood there, looking drained and still wiping the tears from her eyes. Hannah wanted to make her peace with Belle and explain all that had happened in the past few hours, but she was transfixed to the spot, thinking 'what can I say, how can I just explain twenty years of lies? I have betrayed my own daughters, especially Belle. I never meant all this to happen, but no one, no one will ever know how a few weeks of frenzied love were the best days of my life.'

Visions of Belle's Father flashed into her mind despite trying to cast them aside. 'I will never tell,' she vowed, 'just how and why it happened, that's all I will tell.' Hannah then said 'Belle.......

Marie again showing that inner strength said,

'Leave it for now Mum, Belle's not ready to hear your excuses or platitudes. You've caused all this heartbreak, do something useful, please look after Andrew whilst I talk with Belle.'

As Mum turned to go out of the bedroom, footsteps were bounding up the stairs, and there in all her beauty stood Lily.

'Whatever is going on Mum, Dad hasn't said a word. No hello Lily love, as he always does. Why is our Belle in bed? Is she ill? What has happened?'

Mum just looked blank, fragile, almost defeated as she made her way down the stairs.

Lily didn't give anyone time to answer, she went on and on as to how the train from Edinburgh had been late and how she nearly missed the only ferry to the island, and that she had been caught in the storm and had had to shelter in the village at GanGan's and Uncle Rob's, another brother on her Dad's side of the family. Anyway I'm here. So what do we do now?'

Marie shouted, 'Oh do shut up Lily, there's been a crisis so just sit down and listen.'

Marie began to relate what had happened over the past twelve hours. Whilst Marie and Lily, heads together in conversation, Belle slipped out of bed and began to get dressed. Marie stopped in the middle of a sentence, alarmed, said,

'What are you doing Belle, you can't possibly be well enough to get up and go out?'

'Where are you going?' whispered Lily, she too having heard most of the story was scared at what Belle might do, and feeling an inward rage at her parents.

Belle retorted ,

'I 'm fine. I'm going to see GanGan Mc Cullum. I am sorry Marie I didn't mean to be so short tempered with you but I have to be on my own and I need to see GanGan.' As Belle grabbed her coat, her Mum came through to the hall and in a quiet voice said,

'Belle we need to talk.'

'Not now Mum, I don't want to talk to you ever. Where is my Dad.?

'He's in milking shed. Where are you going Belle, please.... '

'I am going to see GanGan Mc Cullum.'

Chapter 4

Gan Gan and Grandad lived a mile out of the village in a little cottage which had been their home since they had handed over the farm to Dad. Belle loved her GanGan and knew she would listen and tell her the truth. GanGan loved all their grandchildren and never treated them any differently, but Belle knew instinctively that she was her favourite amongst the eighteen grandchildren.

As Belle sauntered along the road towards the village of Riarch she experienced pain, as she never had before. This wasn't physical pain from her experience in the hideaway and being hauled up cliff face; this was raw pain in her heart and mind. How could Mum have betrayed her all those years? How could Dad be having an affair with her at number sixteen. Damn it she was about the same age as our Marie. It made Belle's stomach turn over at the very thought.

As she approached Village Street she saw Uncle Callum coming out his cottage with his two youngest boys, her cousins, fifteen-year-old Jamie and fourteen year old Colin. Looked like they were going to play football or perhaps going to the local match on the new sports field. Of course, Belle suddenly remembered that Riarch had got through to the finals in the Islands Tournament. Everyone would be on their way to watch and cheer their team, all of them local boys.

Riarch Billies had never reached the finals in its history and of course her twin brothers would be playing. Belle wondered if they had arrived from the mainland yet. She thought could she face her brothers who would know something was amiss and no doubt had heard of her rescue? Had they heard what had gone off at home?

Uncle Callum spied his favourite niece and shouted to her,

"Eh lass what are you doing wandering through Riarch? You surely should still be taking it easy. Why did you go down the cliff face Belle? What's gone on at home, everyone seems so angry?

He had a quick flash of memory of twenty odd years ago; as quick as that memory came back to him he dismissed it.

Belle thought I should say thanks but she felt such a sense of desolation that she couldn't form the words, only to say

'I cannot tell you. Ask Mum and Dad. Anyway I'm fine Uncle Callum, am on my way to see GanGan and Grandad'

'Well. Lass if you feel up to it come and cheer on the lads. It's a big day for Riarch' Jamie and Colin looked anxious to be off so Belle murmured,

'Well I might just do that.'

As Belle left the village daydreaming or rather reliving her nightmare she could hear a lot of hollering coming towards her: of course the football fans were shouting "up the Billies, up the Billies."

There were a good few cars coming towards her probably come across from the mainland on the ferry. There were only a handful of cars on Riach. Their horns blasting as the sheep and their lambs were wandering on the road. As the crowds drew closer Belle could see her two brothers with Grandad. Such a sight of colour, all wearing the red and black of the Wallace Tartan Scarves, supporting their team. The twins looked a little anxious and after making sure that Belle was okay, they were off. Apparently the ferry was late on landing, nothing new. The twins would have to move quickly as they had to change and sike themselves up for the match.

After promising that she might come and see the second half of the game Belle espied the landmark of the island, Grandad and GanGan's television mast. You could see it anywhere on the island. They had been the first to have television. Their children had clubbed together over Christmas to buy the set, although thrilled, no one really watched the programmes a great deal as the reception was poor with the screen giving off the impression of a snowstorm. When Grandad turned the set on, fiddling with the knobs to get a decent picture, you could always hear him swearing in Gaelic.

Belle was now about five hundred yards from the cottage, she saw Fred coming towards her. His real name was Friederick Braun, a German pilot who had been shot down during the war. He had been a prisoner of war and had never returned to his native Germany, no one ever knew why. After the end of the war he came to the island looking for work. He had a rough passage with the islanders, but soon they began to accept him as a person and not a German. He had changed his name by deed poll to Fred Buchanen and married Meg Dalgleish. She was ten years his senior and they were blessed with two girls, both at the Infant School.

Fred shouted,

'Belle, I heard that you had fallen down Bix Top Face? Are you all right, how did it happen and you just home for a holiday.'

Belle thought, Oh no, he is the last person I want to see.

'Hullo Fred, it was an accident and I am really okay, just a few cuts and bruises. I really must be off as I have come up to see GanGan. Are you off to the final? I 'll probably see you there later.'

'All right Belle, I'll tell Meg and the girls I've seen you. Pop across and see the girls before you leave the island.'

Belle, thought what a good actress I am with others. She took the path on the left that led to a hillock where she felt she could gather her thoughts together before seeing GanGan. As she sat down, she noticed that the grass was a little damp, but she didn't care. Her problems were momentarily put aside as her gaze wandered to Riarch , a truly beautiful village with its higgledy piggley cottages. Just in front of her feet rabbits were scurrying down their burrows. To the East stood The Infant School where she along with rest of family had started their early learning. The school from this angle looked like it had been plonked down on top of raised platform. The senior school was just an extension of four rooms to the Infants whilst at the rear of the school were the playing fields and here she could see crowds of fans shouting their heads off in support of their teams.

There was music being played. sounded like the pipes and a brass band. Normally, Belle thought she would have been thrilled to be part of the excitement and the thrill of seeing Riarch Billies play their game, but no she had too much on her mind.

It was quite warm for March as the sun shone its blessing on Riarch. Dotted around were gorse bushes with their yellow mantle of colour.

To the West, a complete contrast. The Spearan hills today looked grey. So often they seemed to change colour depending on the weather. A mist seemed to be hanging over Spearan which gave the impression that a table had been placed on summit. It looked rather forbidding. As youngsters they had never attempted to climb Spearan as it was deemed unsafe. This was something else her Dad had instilled in them, particularly her twin brothers.

The island in its very nature was one of continually changing scenes. In winter it was stark, in spring colour and new life. The lambs were frolicking just a few hundred yards from GanGan's cottage. In summer a fragrance of flowers one never experienced in the city. In autumn that was when Spearan looked at its best as late heather bloomed all over the mountain.

The varying colours just looked as if a cape had been thrown over mountain.

Chapter 5

Riarch was only a small island and the village had been deemed the capital. She smiled as she thought of Newcastle. No comparison. Riarch Village was home to almost seven hundred people with another three hundred scattered in cottages throughout the island. People made their living either in sheep and cattle, fishing or the spinning of wool. Most young people left the island, as there was little future for them if they stayed put. Nevertheless island life had vibrancy, colour and a tremendous community spirit. The school catered for children and young people up to the age of sixteen after which they had to go to the mainland for further education, just as her twin brothers had done. The pub and the Kirk were central to life with in the community.

Beyond Riarch Village she could see the McCullum Farmstead, with its many outbuildings for the animals. Dad had twenty Highland Cattle, the only cattle who could survive the tough island weather conditions. They were the pride of his life. There were also a large flock of sheep that wandered all over and at present it was the middle of the lambing season. This was a busy time when most of the McCullum family and other hired hands came and gave a hand with all the lambs.

Belle's eyes were drawn to Bix Top Face. She shuddered, what had been her favourite place now brought tremors of fear to her mind. How close she had been to losing her life and it was all Mum's fault. But was it? How would GanGan react? Would she condemn Belle's Mum? GanGan would know what to do after all her and Grandad had brought up five boys and two girls. Belle despite her injuries from her experience on Bix Top Face and the pain deep within her soul, felt more ready to meet with her beloved

GanGan who would be on her own as the rest of household had gone to the match.

As she approached the cottage the scent of the many spring flowers from the garden seemed to just waft around Belle. She had never really noticed before what a lovely scene the cottage made with the wildness of the countryside around it. The spring flowers, yellows, whites, pinks and different greens seemed to speak of a gentleness which reached out to Belle whilst the grazing pastures with their unkempt look gave her courage, yes even boldness to ask GanGan all the questions which were swirling around in her brain. Did she know about Mum's affair during the war years? Did she know who fathered Belle? Was it true about Dad? As Belle approached the back door of the cottage, she was feeling a feverish anticipation that all her problems would be solved.

She could hear GanGan singing some Gaelic tune for she loved her native language and singing was part of her heritage. Gan Gan loved and never tired to tell the stories of the times when her own Dad had been a singer in his young days often performing in public houses and clubs on the mainland.

When Belle saw GanGan she felt the tears streaming down her face as GanGan held her tight. GanGan was still an attractive woman, even though she was coming up seventy years of age. Her hair at one time had been a raven colour and was now peppered with white, and as far as Belle could recall it had always been in a bun, looking like a ball at the nape of her neck. GanGan looked flustered as she had been baking all morning for the lads in the football team, and as she sat down she let out a sigh saying,

'Aw Belle lass, what made you go down BixTop Face Cliff and risk losing your life? Eh, c'mon lass tell GanGan. Are you in trouble; is it a lad? Marie brought shame on the family, well that is what your Dad says, but I don't think so, she made a mistake and that little bairn of hers is a fine lad.'

Belle words were clipped as she said,

'Gangan if anyone else asks me why I went down Bix Top Face again I shall scream. I didn't plan it. It is not my fault. Sorry GanGan I am so fed up and I feel as if someone has kicked me in the stomach. It's all Mum's fault.'

GanGan didn't say a word and thought this lovely lass with her brown velvety eyes should not be in such pain of heart. She looked so pale. Her eyes were puffy, it was obvious she had been crying. She is so different from the other bairns, and how she resembles our Callum when he was a lad.

Of all her grandchildren Belle was the one who thought carefully about everything and was always there for her Grandad and herself. Bairns, she thought when they reached teenage years seemed to grow apart from their grandparents, but not Belle. She never missed an opportunity to come and see them and also her Mum's parents who lived on the other side of the island. Yes, Belle was a very sensitive young lass.

GanGan was suddenly aware that Belle was going on about her Mum and Dad having a row. This made GanGan sit up and listen intently to her granddaughter. When Belle had finished sharing every detail of the events, she just burst into tears. Her GanGan was in a state of utter shock. She got up slowly and put more peat logs on the fire, and then put the blackened kettle on top to make a cup of tea, whilst thinking, surely Belle's got it wrong. She has misheard. Admittedly Belle was the odd one only in colouring and stature, but there again Callum had been the odd one amongst her own brood. All her daughter-in-law's side had been fair skinned with blond, almost white hair. This big secret which Hannah had locked away never to be shared for all those years was indeed threatening to cause division with their families.

Tea now made GanGan asked Belle,

'Are you sure you heard correctly Belle lass?'

It was true that Hannah had always said 'Our Belle is a throwback to previous generations.' It was a sort of joke in the family, never said with any malice. Belle said,

'Everything I have told you GanGan is true, what am I to do?'

'The first thing we are going to do is that we will make our way to the football match, I promised your Grandad and brothers that I would bake some scones and cakes for the teams, so that is where we are going and I will have a think about what you have told me, then we will talk again'

Belle knew that this was how GanGan dealt with problems and daren't question her, even though she herself felt so desperate for answers. As they picked up the baskets of cakes and scones GanGan kissed Belle and promised her things would work out. They stepped out of the cottage into brilliant sunshine that seemed to lighten their steps. Although it was sometimes cool in March today was an exception, with everything looking so fresh after the storm and a light warm breeze drifted with them as they ambled towards Riarch village.

GanGan could see her youngest son Rob coming up the brae. He was supposed to have come half an hour a go to help with the baskets.

'You're late Rob, its a good job Belle's come to help me.'

Uncle Rob was Belle's favourite uncle. For one he wasn't as old as the others. He was the same age as Marie. GanGan had given birth to Rob when she was almost forty-six years old so she had a special place for her youngest.

Rob was chattering about the match saying that Riarch Billies were leading by one goal and that it was a fantastic match. Half time would be in about ten minutes so we'd better hurry Rob was saying and urging his Mum and Belle on at the same time. Needless to say the scones and cakes disappeared within seconds of the half-time whistle being blown. GanGan was very quiet and seemed to be elsewhere rather than listening to her son's and grandsons excited words on the match. Grandad asked if she was okay. Belle too was quiet but inwardly having a sense of peace as she chatted with Dougie and Duncan whose faces were aglow as it had been Dougie who had scored the leading goal. Duncan pleaded with Belle to stay for the second half, so she agreed to stay only if the Riarch Billies stayed in the lead.

Chapter 6

GanGan said she would get off home and start preparing the tea; she urged Belle to stay with Rob. As Belle turned round to wave to GanGan she saw her Dad. He was on his own and looked rather anxious and a bit forlorn. He espied Belle and began to weave his way through the crowds of supporters towards his daughter. The local population had been swollen to well over two thousand people, many from the mainland and from neighbouring islands. Riarch had never known so many people to be in one place at any one time.

Alistair, Belle's Dad just stood by his daughter and reached out for her hand. He grasped it tight and tears welled up in his eyes. Belle was so moved as she truly loved her Dad and whatever had happened, in the future nothing would ever change or take away that deep love. She would always have that special relationship. Dad said no words except to mention that he had to return to the farm as the milking had to be done. Lily had promised to help, Hannah being in no fit state to carry the urns. Dad asked Uncle Rob if he could come down to farm after the match and give him a hand.

'You coming to meeting tonight Belle at the Kirk?'

Belle didn't answer his question but told her Dad she would stay with GanGan tonight and return home on Sunday. Belle only had a few days left of her holiday before she had to return to her job as Nanny in Newcastle, thus it was important that to continue to be part of her family she needed to hear the truth from her Mother, even though she had said she never wanted to see her again.

Seeing many of her cousins, family and friends at the match Belle couldn't just slip away back to GanGan's cottage, so she waited until the cheers went up at the end of ninety minutes. Riarch Billies had won the final for the first time in their football history, which had started in 1900 when Queen Victoria was on the throne. Belle remembered how fondly her Great Gran McDonald had spoken of Victoria; in fact she had named one of her daughters after the lady. Folks in Scotland had been proud of their queen as she spent a lot of time in their native land.

Amidst all the cheering, singing, the waving of tartan scarves and the blue and white of the national flag, Belle slipped away from the ground and made her way towards the cottage. She felt a bounce in her step as she remembered Dad gripping her hand. Poor Dad he must be feeling awful. She wondered why Dad had gone to 'her at no 16' was he unhappy at home? For once Belle was not dwelling on her own problems.

As she went into the cottage GanGan already had the meal cooking on the fire. The smell of peat pervaded throughout the cottage, not an unpleasant aroma, giving of a sense of comfort and Belle realized she was in the presence of an assuring love coming from her GanGan, who said to Belle that after the meal we would all be gathering at the Kirk for the regular Lenten Meeting. Belle sighed, and said,

'I just cannot accept this March Madness. To me it is tradition gone crazy. Remember Mum used to cut our hair on 1st March and you did as well. Please GanGan I just cannot face Mum at the meeting, not until I have spoken to her on my own. She's a hypocrite, how can she go to pray when all this has happened. I don't want to see or speak to her, but I know I have to hear the truth and she is the only one who can tell me.'

'Alright lass, you stay with Grandad, and then we will have a walk, if it remains fair weather, up towards The Shillies.'

Belle was relieved and thought the Shillies would be a grand place to be. She remembered the Shillies, so called because the low hills provided a place of shelter for the sheep, but also for courting couples. She had not been there since she had been a teenager when her and Tommy, her then boyfriend had enjoyed their first kiss. She had been all of thirteen. Belle smiled as she remembered Tommy. Their relationship didn't even last two weeks. Tommy was now a serving soldier with The Black Watch. After Tommy there had been Charlie, he was sixteen and he had tried it on, fumbling in places not allowed, but his kissing was really something, sent tingles through her whole body. Poor Charlie he had joined the Dawson family trawler business when he was eighteen, and the boat went down in rough seas off Norway. All hands had been lost. For Belle it was good to remember all these different instances, which brought a smile, warm feelings and sadness as well. This was much better that the hot rage she had experienced earlier in the day.

Grandad and Uncle Rob returned from the triumphant match and behind them the twins. Rob said he would have a quick bite along with the twins then go down to the farmhouse and give Alistair a hand with the animals. GanGan served her favourite meal, Haggis and Neaps, strange really as we always had this on Burns Night when the whole community met in the school for a supper to remember Scotland's Famous Bard, Robbie Burns. Uncle Rob had been named after Robbie Burns. GanGan was strange at times; in fact the whole island community had some strange practices. This was another of the March Madness Traditions, one which most of us didn't understand, but just accepted.

After GanGan had gone to Kirk and the others to the farm, Belle washed the pots. She made her way through to the living room to be with her Grandad, who was fiddling with the knobs of the television. It was hard work watching as the screen gave off its usual snowstorms, though you could hear the words being spoken. It sounded like the news and Belle pricked up her ears when she heard the newsreader announce that George Formby, the comedian and singer had died. He was known as the Lancashire Lad. She thought immediately of her employers who were great Formby fans. They would travel as far as Liverpool or London to hear him.

Another piece of news was that the USSR had launched a rocket containing a dog and that it had landed safely. Grandad was muttering to himself, 'whatever is the world coming to, launching a dog in a rocket.' He seemed so disgusted that he turned off the television and turned on the wireless. As the music was blaring out, Grandad's favourite programme, the football scores, a Saturday night ritual, were about to come on. He never seemed to win anything but silence reigned in the household as the newsreader read out the results. Belle observed her Grandad. He was still a handsome upright man with silver hair now thinned, and the deepest of cobalt eyes, which always seemed to hold a twinkle and a smile. Her Dad resembled Grandad, although Dad was a bit taller.

She was struck how many of her family had blue eyes of different shades and here was Belle with brown eyes. When she mulled this over the dark depression enveloped her, as she remembered her mother's word. 'Our Belle is a throwback to previous generations,' she wasn't a throwback at all just someone else's child, the father who must have had brown eyes.

Belle came out of her anguished reverie when GanGan came in. Grandad asked'

'Had a good meeting Fi?' Fi was short for Fiona and Grandad had always called his wife Fi.

'Aye, the same as usual,' said GanGan not giving away anything.

'C'mon lass let's away up to the Shillies.'

Despite being March it was quite a pleasant evening, although darkness wasn't far away, the sun dipped over the horizon as they wandered up to The Shillies. GanGan simply said,

'Go and see your Mum tomorrow and allow her to tell you the whole story.'

'Do you know the truth GanGan?'

'No lass, it is between you, your mum, sisters and your Dad, there is no mileage in feeling bitter and angry, all I want is for you to forgive the wrongs done to you.'

Belle was now perilously close to tears but managed to control herself as she felt such love for her GanGan and Grandad and such loathing for her Mum. She was like a yoyo loving one minute and hating the next.

As darkness fell, the full moon was low in the sky. It was known as the tidal moon and was always bright and clear, such an awe inspiring sight. Even the stars appeared to be twinkling their lights of hope as GanGan and Belle began to make their way back to the cottage. Before going to Gangan's comfy bed in the spare room, Belle sat by the open window, gazing out into the darkness with the clouds scudding across in front of the moon. Rain began to fall gently, pattering on the open window. Before closing the window Belle listened to the bleating of the sheep and lambs wandering around outside the cottage continually munching the grass. They never seemed to stop eating. She thought it is a good job Grandad has a wall round his garden as in the morning there would be no flowers or vegetables left. With the dampness of the night the scents of the flowers and gorse seemed stronger than normal.

Belle's last thoughts before falling asleep were that her life in a few short hours had been crushed into thousands of pieces, and she wondered if those pieces would ever be put together again. GanGan had told her gently to pray before going to sleep, well she didn't think that would help her tomorrow when she went home as she didn't believe God answered prayers, especially hers, so what was the use.

Chapter 7

Next morning Belle arrived at the farm at half past nine, and as she went to the back door, she nearly did an about turn, but Lily had seen her coming down the lane. Lily shouted Belle and gave her a hug. For Lily tears came easily and she was weeping buckets, not a lot of help to Belle as she tried to keep reign of her own emotions. Then Andrew was tottering towards Belle with his arms up in the air. Belle lifted him and held him tight, thinking to herself 'you and me are in the same boat. We don't know our Dads'. Belle could hear voices coming from the direction of the front kitchen. This was where meals were taken, having been cooked in the back kitchen.

'Mum, why have you never told Belle? Why have you always said she was a throwback? Such cruel words. Why, Mum? What have you done to Belle?'

Marie was now shouting at her mother.

Hannah suddenly turned on Marie screaming,

'What right have you to question me about what happened in my life, when you yourself had a child, and you not married? We have had to live with the shame. 'Just what right have you?' raged Hannah, 'you know nothing….nothing.'

Marie retorted, 'Live with what shame yours or mine?'

Belle still holding Andrew with Lily following walked into the kitchen. Marie seemed as if she was still shaking with temper, but seeing her son, she began to calm down. A knock came at the back door and Lily went to open the door and there stood Gran McDonald, Mum's mother. She was known by the family as Gran Mary.

'Hullo Lily, I heard you were all home and that Belle had had an accident on BixTop Face, so thought it's a nice day, got the old bike out and come over.

It's taken me half an hour and a cup of tea would be welcome.'

By now Mum had calmed down a little and acknowledged her mother.

'You look peaky Hannah, doing too much on the farm no doubt. I've told you for years that your place is in the house, and that Alistair should employ someone full time. Didn't that German what's his name help you in the past?'

'Oh Mum don't keep saying that German. He is now an islander and had his name changed by deed poll, for goodness sake he is married to one of ours. Anyway if that's all you've come over to say you might as well go home.'

Marie came downstairs with Andrew and said hullo to her other Gran, knowing that she disapproved of her and Andrew Her Gran Mary, had made it quite clear whilst she was pregnant with Andrew of the shame she had brought to her family. As she looked at Marie, Mary thought thank goodness her name is Mc Cullum and not Mc Donald. Of course she wouldn't say that to the girl.

'Hullo Marie, where's our Belle?

'She is playing with Andrew upstairs; she will be down in a minute. Lily let's go and make some toast and tea, Andrew needs to have his breakfast.'

Marie and Lily went to the back kitchen; this was where it was cosy and all the cooking took place on an open fire with ovens at either side. When Mum and Dad had taken over the farm, the first thing they did was to have a new Triplex fire built in to the far wall.

Marie had always had a short fuse and was now absolutely fuming, 'Why is Gran Mary so mean and spiteful Lily? GanGan Mc Callum never says things like she does, and she is never spiteful. I don't like her one bit, in fact I hate her' Lily's thoughts were the same, but she wanted to keep the peace for Belle's sake, so she suggested,

'I know Marie, why don't we have some breakfast and put Andrew in his pushchair and ask Gran Mary if she wants to come to the village to see that new second hand shop. You know how she loves looking at bric a brac. That way it would give Mum and Belle time to chat. I think we have both said what we wanted to

Mum. Anyway we cannot be mad at Mum anymore, well I know I can't. Do you think Gran Mary knows anything Marie?'

'Don't know,' Marie answered, 'and I don't really care, she is just an old busy body. She is so flipping perfect and makes out that she is better than us, and I don't like it when she starts getting at Dad. Did I hear Gran say something about Fred Buchanen?'

'Yes, she called him a German and Mum was furious. I like Fred, he was real kind to us when we were younger. Do you remember when he brought Duncan home after he had fallen off his bike and cut his head open. He always helped Dad on the farm and never expected payment, that was before he married Meg. Yes I think Gran is always interfering. Anyway let's ask her about going to village.'

The girls took the tea and toast through to the kitchen, the place where all the arguments had taken place when they were children and it had also served as the problem solver sitting around a well scrubbed table big enough to seat twelve. There had been lots of fun and laughter in those days. Belle was holding

Andrew, Mum was sitting wringing her hands and Gran Mary was looking out the window. There was silence, except for Andrew chattering.

The silence was shattered by the slam of the kitchen door. Dad was taking off his boots in the lobby and shouting for Lily to make him a cup of tea. He had to be quick as he had two ewes having a difficult birthing. As he walked into kitchen his eyes just filled when he saw Belle. He ignored Gran and Hannah. He took a step towards Belle and she burst into tears and fell into his open arms. Marie and Lily too, were upset to see their Dad's tears. Gran with all her spite said,

'Have we another bastard to be born into the family?'

There was mayhem for a few moments. Andrew screaming, Mum shouting at her Mum, Dad's rage was almost out of control until his three girls together said,

'Dad stop it, stop it.'

Hannah screamed at her mother,

'Get out, you hateful nasty old hussy. Don't come back to the farm again.'

Gran Mary stormed out and almost tripped over Dad's boots. She too was shouting to Hannah,

'You already wed and carrying on like a common whore. Yes, Hannah I know it all. For twenty years you have lied to yourself and left a terrible legacy for our Belle. You should never have got yourself tied up with the McCullum lot. Too many skeletons in their cupboard.'

Utter silence followed her tirade. Dad turned, put on his boots and moved quickly out of the house, away to the lambing sheds before anyone could say a word. The three girls stood open mouthed still hearing Gran Mary's spiteful loaded words. Andrew by now was eating toast and trying to catch Bess and Tess's tail.

Hannah ran out of the house and started following her Mum. Gran Mary was on her bike and was pedaling furiously down the road. She could hear Hannah shouting, so she put on her brakes and waited until Hannah now breathless from running caught her up.

'Mum please Mum wait, with a sob almost taking her words, I am sorry for what I said, but my family is falling apart all because of me keeping a secret for twenty years. How did …..'

Cutting her short, Mary said,

'You were our only daughter, but you have brothers who told me snippets about what you were doing. Did it never occur to you that carrying on with that lad who just used girls for his own end you would get hurt? You already with two bairns, how could you Hannah? Ah I know your answer, you were in love. Mamby pamby rubbish. He should have joined up like the rest of the lads in Riarch. All the excuses his mother made about him having a weak chest.'

A fear was mounting up in Hannah, if her Mum knew, who else in Riarch had guessed? Her mouth was trembling, tears rolling down her cheeks, she sank to the ground. What had she done?

Gran Mary, as she was known in family, could no longer hold back, as she too sat on the ground and held Hannah closely, whispering words of love, just as she had done when Hannah was a little girl.

'I am sorry Hannah, I did not mean to call you a whore. May God forgive me? Let us go back to the house; the girls need to know the truth, especially Belle. C'mon lass. You have to face each one of them now.'

Marie was tending to Andrew when her Mum and Gran Mary walked in. Marie longed to take a swipe at these two women who were unfortunately related to her but this would upset Andrew. She took her son and quickly ran upstairs. Her Mum in a weary voice asked her where Lily and Belle had gone.

'They've gone to help our Dad with the lambs.'

Chapter 8

Lily and Belle found their Dad in the shed sitting on a bale of straw, stroking the Collie pups, whilst crying his eyes out. They could hear the cry of newborn lambs and Dad looked utterly exhausted, as he had to struggle to bring two sets of twins into the world. Both girls rushed over to him and they held on to each other without saying any words. Gran Mary's spiteful words had hurt and Belle thought they are just stupid lies. She never liked our family, took every opportunity to humiliate Dad and, particularly Marie since she had given birth to Andrew. She even thought that I had got myself into trouble with a lad. How could she say 'is there another bastard to born into the family,' how could she? She has the mind of a sewer. What can I do to pay her back thought Belle as she tried to shut out the terrors of the past hours that were etched on her mind?

Dad gently pushed away his girls and said,

'I am so sorry. I never meant you to be hurt in this way.' As he tried to speak Lily gave out a high-pitched scream.

'What is it Lass, what's the matter?'

'A rat' said Lily. 'I saw a big black rat, look over there, go on look by that loose straw.'

As a youngster she had always been terrified of rats and mice. Before Dad could say anything Bess and Tess were now barking madly and chasing the wind. The rat had disappeared. Dad stood up wearily and said to Lily who had now calmed down and to Belle,

'Let's go into the house and try sort out this terrible mess.'

As they left the lambing sheds, the skies were darkening, no doubt another storm. Belle shuddered and started to run towards the back door to be met by Marie with Andrew strapped into his pushchair.

'Where are you going Marie?' asked Dad.

'I am going to village as I promised to meet with Jo for a drink and a bit of dinner.' Jo had been Marie's friend from school and their closeness had continued, even though Marie now had Andrew. Jo was getting married in June so they had loads to talk about as Jo hoped that Andrew would be a pageboy at her wedding, even though he was only a toddler.

'But Marie you need to be here so that we can all be together to try to pick up the smashed pieces of this family.'

'No Dad this is between you, Mum and Belle. Anyway I don't want to be near Mum or Gran, I do not trust myself. I might just bash them both, I am that bloody mad. You all need to chat without us. Are you coming down to village Lily, Jo won't mind.'

Dad looked aghast at Marie, saying, ' mind your language lass,' then whispered, 'may God forgive me.'

'No Marie I'll do some jobs for Dad. The sheep and the lambs need tending. I'll potter around and I am expecting Craig to phone at half past one, so I need to be here.' Despite all that had happened in a couple of days, which seemed like weeks, when Lily mentioned Craig's name her eyes shone. She was in love.

Dad looked up at the threatening clouds, they looked as black as thunder.

'You'd better be quick Marie, it's going to pour down any minute.'

As Marie, almost running with the pushchair towards the village to meet Jo, Lily went back to the lambing shed and Belle linked her arm through Dad's as they made their way to the house. Opening the back door they could hear voices, which sounded like Mum and Gran.Mary's Belle felt she couldn't face her Gran but Dad whispered,

'We'll sort it out lass.'

'Mother-in-law I would like you to go and help Lily in the lambing shed, so that I can talk with my wife and daughter. If you don't agree you will have to go home and there is a storm brewing so you will get soaked to the skin.'

Gran Mary looked so subdued; she nodded her head, donned her coat and hat and made for the back door, shutting it rather loudly. As she made her way across to the lambing shed, the storm was picking up speed, as trees seemed to be bending over almost to breaking point. She found Lily cradling two newborn lambs, her eyes glistening with tears. Mary feeling rather embarrassed at her previous outburst, waited a few seconds before going over into the warmth of the lambing pen beside Lily.

Lily completely ignored her Gran Mary, got up placing the lambs back with their mother; she went further down the shed where some ewes were starting their labour. Her thoughts were going round in ever increasing circles of confusion. She wasn't keen on Gran Mary, as she had always been so strict, yet she had been there in emergencies and had cared for the family, especially as her Mum had said when Dad was away at the war. Why had she been so spiteful towards her own daughter and to Dad?

Belle looked at her Mother seeing the pain and shame in the face she thought she had loved for twenty years, and now could only feel a mixture of love and hate. She remembered GanGan's words not to harbour bitterness. Of course deep down she loved her mother. All she wanted was to know the truth. There was a moment of awkwardness between the three of them but it passed as Dad 's voice came to Belle,

'Hannah why are we in this mess? Three months ago we were celebrating our twenty-five years of marriage, and we even went to the Kirk to receive a blessing. What hypocrites we are. Look at the torment in our Belle's face.'

Hannah staring into the flames of the fire, spoke in a hushed angry voice,

'Twenty-five years, so what were you doing with her at number sixteen. You living two lives, this is not all about me is it Alistair?

'Woman you never gave me a chance to explain..'

'What is there to explain,' Hannah retorted, 'even my own Mother knew something was going on between you two, and her the same age as our Marie. I knew when you came home every Thursday smelling of cheap scent, certainly not what I use.'

'What is it you want Hannah? What do you want me to do?'

'Take responsibility for your actions,' Hannah retorted.

There was a spark of deep anger in Alistair's eyes when he said, 'for years you have shared my bed and making love was like having an ice maiden. It's no good shaking your stupid head, it is as I say. You have never shown me passionate love, whereas Beth, yes Beth is her name, has welcomed me, loved me and respected me, age does not matter.

Belle sitting listening, her mind in turmoil, felt something snap in her head and began to scream abuse at her parents.

'Both of you are disgusting, how can you be my parents or you at least Mum. I hate you both, all your concerned about is lying to each other. What about you Mum, giving birth to an illegimate child, eh what about me? I am that child.' With tears streaming down her face Belle shouted, 'who is my father? I have a right to know. I will find out as I am going to ask Gran Mary, she will tell me'

As Belle rushed out slamming the back door and feeling such pains in her head she almost collided with Lily.

'Belle, please Belle stop, what on earth is going on? Lily caught her sister in her arms and just held her as she sobbed. Tell me Belle, let me help, how I dislike this family.

'I need to see Gran Mary, she knows the identity of my father, I have to know,' cried Belle. 'Where is she Lily, tell me.'

'Gran Mary is in the lambing shed, I don't want anything to do with her, and she is an old hag.'

Belle for a moment was amazed at Lily's words but old hag or not she had to see her. She left Lily standing with a non-plussed expression on her face and went to find Gran Mary. She stopped dead in her tracks as she heard male voices coming up the lane and as they drew nearer she recognized her twin brothers. The threatened storm had passed so they were taking their time. Belle thought, oh not now please as she escaped into the lambing shed and found Gran Mary in tears, holding a newborn lamb.

'Ah Belle, lass I am so sorry for all this trouble and pain you are suffering. I am a spiteful old woman and have only made things worse between your Mum and Dad. Please Belle sit down and let us chat, I tried to talk to Lily but she wouldn't have anything to do with me and went off in a huff.'

'Gran Mary, who is my father? That woman you called a whore in the kitchen who is supposed to be my mother will not tell me, as she is too busy accusing Dad of having an affair with Beth Matthews. Who is my father Gran Mary?'

'Come lass, sit on this bale of straw with me and I will tell you a story. The first thing you need to know Belle is that you are loved.'

'Loved? By whom I wonder,' said Belle.

'Now don't interrupt, as the story will never be told. There was a war on and Alistair your supposed

65

Dad was serving with The Gordon Highlanders and was fighting in France, that was in the backend of 1939 just after the war started. He didn't come home on leave until May 1940. He had already had a spell in hospital with a smashed leg and that is why he still limps. Marie was already coming up three and Lily almost two years old. When he came home he was depressed and not the easiest of men to live with, but your Mum nursed him back to health and he returned to his unit at the beginning of July.'

' Gran Mary I only want to know who is my father, not a life story' Belle said wearily.

'Just listen child; it is important that you know the entire story. When your step dad was away at war your Mum fell in love with another man, she was lonely and trying to bring up two small children on her own and help to run the farm. She was absolutely terrified that anyone find out so she ended the affair, but she never stopped loving your real father, even now I know she is still deeply in love with him. You were born in the March of 1941; nine months after your step dad's leave so everyone assumed that he was your father. I know your Mum always said you were a throwback to a previous generation, now I realize that those words covered her affair with your real father. It took me sometime to realize that you were someone else's bairn. Yes Belle, your Mum knew that you were born to her lover, but tried to cover it up for the sake of family and your step dad. I am just so sorry you had to find out the way you did lass.'

'But who is he Gran' whispered Belle.

'Your Mam has to tell you that, it would be wrong for me to reveal his name. You know that Belle, just calm yourself down now and go and ask your Mum. She is in as much pain as you are as she sees her family collapse around her. Belle before you decide thanks for trusting me, and I will support each of you as we mend our lives together. I am also sorry for what I said about Marie. That was an evil thing to utter.'

Gran Mary now made a move to the doors of the lambing shed when the twins rushed in, with Duncan shouting, 'where is Belle, what have you said Gran Mary, why don't you just go home. Why have you been interfering in our lives? Why? Lily has told us everything and how you called Mum and Marie names.'

Dougie started to vent his anger when Belle in a firm voice said, 'enough is enough, please both of you say no more. Let me sort out my problems with Mum, don't interfere and leave Gran Mary alone now.'

The boys taken aback at Belle's words found themselves a wee bit isolated and bewildered as they wandered off towards the village asking each other what had happened in so short a time to break up their family. Nearing the centre of Riarch, they spied Marie coming out the coffee shop with Andrew and her friend Jo.

Dougie called to Marie as she turned to make her way to Gangan's. 'Wait a minute Marie' as she said goodbye to her friend she was quite amazed to see her brothers. She thought that they would be back on the mainland whooping it up as they normally did at the weekend. Both of them looked down at the mouth, so she teased them saying,

'What's up having no luck with the girls?'

Duncan just looked at her and spoke quietly, 'we have been home and it was like hell on earth with Mum and Dad shouting and bawling at each other. Lily not speaking to either of them and our Belle looked drawn and pained and she told us that she would sort out her own problems and not to be rude to Gran Mary. Lily has given us a run down of what has been going on. Is it all true Marie? Is Belle only our half-sister? Who is her dad Marie? Why has no one told us anything? Is that why Belle went up to Bix Top Face.'

'Hang on both of you, so many questions. Yes, it is all true and Gran Mary, the old hag has not helped, in fact she stirred it all up. Now we too must not interfere and just allow Mum and Dad time to sort out their problems and for Belle to be able to spend time with Mum'

Marie felt sorry for her brothers; they were only seventeen and should be on top of the world instead of feeling so let down. She said,

'why don't we all go to GanGan and Grandad's for an hour. We should go and see them more anyway, and they do love to see Andrew. You know they have never judged me for having Andrew outside marriage. Come on you two let's hurry as there could be another lot of rain to come.'

Chapter 9

Meanwhile Lily was anxious as she went back to the house as she expected Craig to phone her, but she did wonder if she would be intruding in the conversation that would take place between Belle and her Mum. Some holiday this was, she wished was back at the hospital and then felt guilty as her family really should come first. Why did all this have to happen in such a short space of time. She opened the back door and heard the phone ringing, this must be Craig. Belle was already answering when Lily rushed indoors and handed the phone over to Lily. She said it was okay as she and Mum was in the back kitchen, so not to worry about chatting to Craig.

Dad had gone back to the lambing shed and Gran Mary had decided to return home in between the showers so Belle and Mum had complete privacy. At first nothing was said, only the hissing of the kettle on the fire could be heard. Belle looked at her Mum and thought how ill she seemed. The revelations of the last few hours had taken its toll not only on her but also on Belle. Her Mum whispered,

'I am so sorry Belle that you had to find out in the way you did.'

'Would you ever have told me Mum?'

'No I don't think so Lass, as nothing would have been gained by the telling of a secret I had held in my heart for twenty years, one which I really began to believe. But now that it's out I feel relieved but pained at what I have done to you.'

I fell in love with your real Dad during war time, it was a whirlwind romance, but I ended the affair quickly when I knew I was pregnant with you.'

Belle then asked her Mum in a quiet voice, 'did you know whose baby it was?'

'Yes' her Mum replied. 'as soon as you were born it was confirmed as you are very like the one I loved. I did love your now step dad, but in a different way, but not with the passion that I experienced with your Dad.

In a hushed tone Belle asked, 'Who is my Dad'

There was another silence, Mum sighed and said, 'your Uncle Callum.'

Belle felt light headed and thought she would pass out as it was quite hot in the back kitchen, so she got up, going over to the sink and let the cold water tap run so she could splash her face and have a drink. Still she didn't say anything, feeling all the pent up anger just slip away. Her Mum was sobbing and Belle felt moved to go and put her arms around this sad woman. She reminded herself of Gangan's advice, not to hold bitterness.

'Does Uncle Callum know that I am his child?'

'No Belle, I never told him as I knew it would damage my marriage and your now step dad loved you so much. At the time I thought I was doing the right thing and soon after your Uncle Callum was married.

I don't expect you will be able to forgive me Belle, but please do not stop loving your family or us. I will have to tell Uncle Callum as he will find out soon enough. I need to have time to think it through. Then there is your now step dad..

'No' Belle said with vehemence. 'He is my Dad and always will be. I love him with all my heart and now there is brokenness between you. What is going to happen to you both Mum? Can you forgive Dad for going to Beth Matthews? Can you Mum?'

'I am going to try to sort out our problems. I knew this when we had our marriage blessed and I have to be true to my faith,'

For a moment Belle thought what pious words you speak Mum, it is all meaningless. She felt she was being rather selfish with this sort of thinking. They could all start again, could they not.?

Uncle Callum is my Dad, it could have been worse, he rescued me from Bix Top Face and he has always looked on me as his favourite niece. All of a sudden she felt terrified as well as awkward. How would she react when she saw Uncle Callum? This was such a strange happening but nothing could alter the past. Belle's thoughts were all jumbled in her mind and she felt so painfully exhausted. She could faintly hear her Mum's voice, asking her,

'Belle I do love you, shall we start again?'

This moment was lost as Lily and Dad both came into the back kitchen together. Lily, looking embarrassed at her intrusion said she was going to see Gangan. She was off so quickly that no one had a chance to say anything.

Dad approached his darling Belle whom he loved so much that it hurt and just held her close, their tears mingling, no words needed. Belle whispered to him, 'you will always be my Dad.'

Belle realized just how weary she felt so she slipped out and made her way upstairs.

Alistair for a moment stood stock still with tears coursing down his face and in a hushed voice uttered, 'Hannah lass, please forgive me, I have so many regrets about the last couple of months. I have made a great mistake and I am not making excuses but I suppose I felt that the love we had for each other had gone cold. Although I knew Belle was not my bairn, I wrongly thought that our love was stronger than any wrongdoing either of us had committed'.

Hannah felt as if all the stuffing had been knocked out of her.

'Oh Alistair it is my wrong not yours that has caused so much hurt. I drove you away with my coldness. Please listen as I tell you the truth. It was during the war years when you were away; I did feel lonely even although I had Marie and Lily. I craved for adult company and I suppose I was bowled over by the attention of Belle's Dad. He was a flirt and I fell for his charm, and in a way I really loved him but it was a lustful love. I t was all to do with sex, he made me feel as if I was the only girl in the world, but as soon as he had his way with me, I realized what I had done. His interest began to fall off and I knew I was pregnant when you came home on leave. I pushed it to the back of my mind until Belle was born. She was so different, like her father. Yes I did always say that she was a throwback to a previous generation, to cover up my own mistake. In the end I almost believed it.'

Alistair took a deep breath saying, 'who was it Hannah?'

'You mean you do not know, how can you not know Alistair? It was your own brother Callum'

'Callum', exploded Alistair, 'did you just say Callum? I'll kill him.'

'No, please Alistair, he does not know, I never told him I was pregnant with Belle. Anyway what good would it do now, only split our family and cause more pain and hurt. Please Alistair, we will have to wait and see what Belle wants. I am sorry, and although these words may sound trite, I do love you. Will you forgive me Alistair?'

Alistair sat with his head in his hands, feeling his whole world was collapsing. How could he look at his brother again, but then it was twenty years ago. It dawned on him that Belle did look like Callum. Did his mother guess, he wondered. Why was Callum the odd one out in his family. Had his mother too made a mistake? All these thoughts were pouring into his mind, circling round and round with no answers.

'Let's leave it for now lass, as the milking needs to be done. Are you coming as I think Lily won't be back in time. The door burst open as Alistair was putting on his boots and there stood his sons, both seemed agitated, angry, and started speaking together, funnily the same words. They had always been close to each other and to their Mum. Alistair wondered if their family would ever recover their love for each other. What about Belle?

'Where is Mum? What have you done Dad? Is it true that you're sleeping with Beth Matthews? How could you Dad? We need to know the truth about our Belle'.

'Not now, shut your mouths; leave your Mum and our Belle alone. It will work out and if they want you to know they will tell you in their own good time. So stop glowering, come and help in the milking shed or go and check the lambs.'

As Hannah came through from the back kitchen she held the boys and said, 'do as your Dad says, please'. In her mind they were children again, when then they were easy to please. Both boys looked uneasy, still angry as they made their way to the sheds.

Chapter 10

$\mathcal{M}$arie and Lily having spent a short time with GanGan and Grandad were on their way back to the farm when they saw Beth Matthews. Lily who never thought wrong of anyone screamed,

'Why did you pick on my Dad, all you are is a common whore'

Marie said 'wheesht Lily, it will be around the village and you still do not know the truth'.

Beth Matthews looked stunned and started going for Lily shouting ,

'Your Dad is great in bed and loves me. I give him what he needs; he can't get enough of me. He is leaving your miserable mother and we're going away off this dead and forsaken island.'

Lily thought what have I done now. She and Marie hurried away stung by the words of Beth Matthews. Was it true that their Dad was leaving? What a mess. Lily knew she would have to tell her Mum and Dad what had taken place in the middle of the village. She wished she hadn't come home. She longed to be off to see Craig.

Marie was stunned by Lily's outburst and was lost in her own thoughts as she pushed the pushchair along the road. Andrew was now fast asleep after his games with GanGan and Grandad. As Marie looked at her son she was very much aware that he looked like his father. She briefly thought will there be problems for Andrew as he grows without knowing his father. As it was it had been a one-night stand after Tom Sullivan's twenty first birthday celebrations, so it had not been an affair as such. Marie recalled her Dad's fury when he found out she was pregnant, she could hear his angry words, 'you're no daughter of mine and you never will be'.

When Andrew was born her Dad had been frosty at first but gradually he had come to love Andrew and was always proud to talk about his grandson to the villagers, although his relationship with Marie was never what it had been before her son's arrival. All these thoughts were crowding Marie's mind as she and Lily approached the farm.

Behind them a man's voice was shouting,

' Just a minute you two loud mouthed hussies, I want a word with you, how dare you scream abuse at my daughter.'

Lily and Marie stood still, amazed at Billy Matthew's tirade. Not knowing what to do or say, they moved slowly backwards. Andrew was now awake, beginning to cry.

Billy Matthew was now shouting, '

'Your father is a dirty old man, who is ruining my Beth's life. I have only been back on the island a few hours to be told that your Dad had seduced my daughter. Where is he, I'll kill him?'

Billy Matthews, a fisherman was a well-built man and also known as a bully who was not scared to use his fists. They said in the village that his wife had died after she had taken another beating, but it was covered up as she had been pregnant at the time. Gossip said she had had a miscarriage. So Beth grew up without the support of her mother and had in the main been left to her own devices. She had few friends and mostly was not all that popular amongst her own age group.

As Billy brushed past the girls, making his way to the back door, Dad appeared from the milking shed, saying,

'What do you want Billy Matthews? Used your fist recently? Looks like you have had a skinful of beer. Behind Dad stood the boys and behind them Mum.

'You have been interfering with my daughter.' shouted Billy, 'She is silly bitch, just like her mother, man mad, but I am not having a dirty old man like you McCallum sully the Matthew's name. You keep away from her or I will kill you.'

There was a complete silence except for Andrew's whimpering. Dad did not move a muscle as he stared ahead into the distance, then Duncan said quietly,

'Get off our land now Mr Matthews, and if you continue to threaten our family we will contact the Police. Take this as a warning, now get off,'

Billy Matthews turned away, to retrace his steps. The family could hear him swearing and also he seemed to be tottering from side to side, obviously the worse for wear with drink.

Mum whispered to Dad, 'will that lass be okay?'

The rest of them were open mouthed as they had heard what their Mum had said, why on earth should she be worrying about Beth Matthews, especially as she was partly responsible for the hurt that each one was experiencing.

Dad nodded his head and made his way back to the milking shed, as did Mum and the boys, each of them lost in their own thoughts. As Lily and Marie went into the kitchen with Andrew toddling behind, Belle met them with a smile. She wore a more confident air and seemed to be at peace with herself and the family as she wrapped her arms around her sisters, saying,

'We can all get on with our lives now, all the secrets are out in the open, well most of them', directing her remarks mainly to Marie.

Marie was about to reply, but Belle went on,

'Do you want to know who my Father is? Can't say I am happy about it as your Dad and my Dad is the only one that I want to call Father.'

Marie and Lily shook their heads in utter disbelief of the calmness of Belle. What had happened in the last few days had been an utter nightmare for everyone, especially Belle, but now the calmness that she wore coloured her sisters mood, until she said,

'My father is Uncle Callum.'

'Uncle Callum,' both the girls exclaimed in amazement. 'Does Dad know? Did Mum tell him? Uncle Callum, surely not.'

They went on and on until Belle said a bit sharply,

'I don't want it spread around the village, it will only cause more rifts in our family, and yes Marie, Lily,

Mum did tell Dad, and furthermore Uncle Callum does not know.'

It was as if the girls could not grasp the truth of their sister had divulged. How could Uncle Callum not know. Even Gran Mary had hinted that she knew of Mum's affair all those years ago. Who else knew they both wondered. Lost in their thoughts, Belle brought them back to reality as she said,

'Please do not discuss this with anyone else, until I have decided the best way to go ahead. I don't want any more hurt to touch the family.'

'It already has, ' Lily said in a glum voice. I had a go at Beth Matthews in the village and called her a whore, and a few folks must have heard what I said and how she replied. Then her drunken father followed us home and has threatened Dad, but he soon gave Billy short shift.'

Belle, like Marie was astounded that Lily, usually so quiet should have such an angry outburst.

'Was it only about Dad, Lily,' asked Belle.

'Yes, nothing else was mentioned, only Dad's affair with Beth and Mum knows all about it now, and I think they have had words with each other. I left them to it and went to bed after my showdown with Mum, as I felt so exhausted.'

A little voice was heard to say 'Mama.' Andrew was demanding his Mum's attention so Belle made her way along with Lily to the lambing sheds where they found the boys helping a struggling ewe to give birth. For once in their lives, they were silent, just looked up at their sisters and carried on with the skills they had learnt as young children, that of the birthing of lambs.

The girls went back to the milking shed and there was Mum doing her usual job, milking, with tears streaming down her face. She tried to hide this from the girls, but it was too late.

'Whatever is the matter Mum,' said Lily. 'Why are you crying, please tell us, we love you.'

Mum rose from her milking stool, straightened her back and took the pail of rich creamy warm milk to the cooler, before saying a word.

'I am so sorry that you have both come home for a holiday and been landed with all this pain. Your

Dad and I have talked and we will continue to do so. We don't intend letting each other go, we have been together too long to allow this break us up. We have forgiven each other, and Belle you too are determining you future. Our family will knit together again provided we are open to one another. I want us to try again.' Just then Marie came into the milking parlour with Andrew, sobbing her heart out. Well this was a surprise as Marie was unusually hard at times and rarely let go of her emotions, only in anger.

'Mum can I have a chat, I need to clear the air with you and Dad.'

Mum and Marie made their way to the house arm in arm with Andrew toddling alone behind them. He was an engaging little boy, and Belle thought, Marie will have to tell him when he is older about his Father. Maybe that is what she was crying about. Dad had now finished in the dairy and he too was going into the house. Well maybe, things will get better now. Lily said as much to Belle as they walked towards the village. The sun in all its glory was falling behind the horizon.

Belle said to Lily, 'I am returning to Newcastle on Thursday, I need to get back to some normality away from the family with all its pressing needs.'

Lily too was thinking of returning to Edinburgh early, but for a different reason...Craig. He was obviously the most important person in her life and she told Belle that they were going to get engaged in the summer. She wanted to move in with Craig but how would her parents and Craig's family react?

Lily said defiantly, 'anyway we are going to do it Belle.'

Belle deep in thought said quietly, 'think it through carefully and follow your heart Lily.'

Lily thought how selfish she was in being so wrapped up in Craig, when Belle had gone through so much pain.

'Belle how do you feel about Uncle Callum being your Dad?'

Nothing really Lily, at least it is still in the family and Mum has told me how it happened. I am not sure if I should challenge Uncle Callum, you see Lily if I do, will it affect him, Sally and the boys? Maybe it is best kept quiet, but you know what its like in a village, someone will find out and that is even worse coming from strangers.'

'I think Belle that you should leave it to Mum and Dad to sort out, after all it is mostly their problem, and it doesn't change your love for them and their love for you, does it?'

As they neared the village Beth Matthews came out of her home, or rather her Father was throwing her out. Her hair was matted in blood, her face puffy, her eyes almost closing. She was now sobbing, it was obvious that her Father had beaten her up. Other neighbours were beginning to gather and some making snide remarks, ' well she got what she deserved. Always hanging around with married men, flaunting herself, just a brazen hussy.'

Lily took pity, the nurse in her overcoming her anger and distaste of Beth Matthews. She put her arm around Beth and made her sit on the village seat whilst Belle told those nosey parkers what to do. Lily said to Beth,

'You are coming home with us, where you will be safe and I can clean you up.'

'Even after I said what I did about your Father, you still want to help me?' sobbed Beth. 'I cannot go to the farm, please help me to get to Fred and Meg Buchanen's, they have always helped me before when Dad has been the worse for drink. I hate him and I am going to leave the island.'

Lily and Belle helped her hobble to the little cottage where Fred, Meg and the girls lived. They were shocked when they saw the state of Beth as Lily and Belle were. She was covered in bruises, not all had been inflicted today thought Lily. Fred was so taken aback that he phoned the local Bobby who happened to be on the island on his monthly visit. In a way Beth was pleased, but still felt guilty as much of it was her own doing, but she knew unless her Father was challenged with his behaviour, he would catch up with her and start the beatings again.

When PC Robbie Macpherson arrived, Beth felt torn in two, trying to decide whether she should tell him the full truth, how her Father sexually abused her, or keep quiet. Stress and the pain of her beating was making her head spin and now she felt so terrified that words wouldn't come when Robbie questioned her. Her inside were churning and she felt sick. He said he would come back in the morning when he would take a statement. He intended to visit Billy Matthews on his way home. Robbie knew he was a heavy drinker and had a record of violence in the past. He needed squaring up after doing that to his own daughter.

Lily and Belle had been shocked to see the extent of Beth's bruising. With the help of Megan they had bathed her gently, hiding their distress and put her to bed in Megan's spare room with a cup of tea laced with brandy. Before they left, Beth called to them and said how sorry she was for saying those terrible accusations about their Dad. Beth falteringly said,

'Your Dad showed me kindness and love, that I had never experienced before. All I have ever known is a good beating from my Dad. I am sad for causing such trouble in your family. When I get over this I am going away to make a decent life for myself.'

Lily and Belle left the cottage with a twinge of unease. Each thinking, how could your Father do that to his daughter? Lily told Belle what had transpired earlier in the day when she had confronted Beth Matthews, which she now truly regretted.

PC Robbie Macpherson hammered on Billy Matthews door, and with no answer he opened the door. No one locked their doors on the island, Robbie thought this may have to change. He found Billy Matthews out cold on the floor with an empty whisky bottle by his side. Robbie went to kitchen, what a mess, dirty pots and pans all over the place. He found a tin jug, filled it with water and poured it over Billy's face. Billy woke up from his drunken stupor, starting to curse and swear; suddenly stopping in mid-sentence when he saw the uniform. He modified his language and asked Robbie why he was here.

'What is it Officer, is it Beth' he asked slurring his words.

'Yes it is Beth, what have you done to her? I'll tell you in case you've forgotten, you beat her black and blue, almost killed her' you're an animal Matthews to do that to your own daughter. What I want to know is what else have you done to her, she is keeping something back, but I will find out when I interview her tomorrow.'

Robbie had three young daughters of his own so he was troubled over Beth, she definitely was hiding something, and he guessed that Billy had been sexually abusing his daughter.

Matthews now looking a little bit startled said, 'She got what she deserved, carrying on with him up at the farm. She is no better than a whore, and she won't talk, otherwise she knows what will happen.'

'You will never threaten your daughter any more Matthews because you are off to the mainland jail on the next ferry, so get yourself ready. I am charging you with grievously bodily harm to your daughter, Beth Matthews.'

Now Robbie was a well-built man but Billy Matthews was a giant of a man, so Robbie had taken precautions in getting some local help, as he knew Matthews would struggle like mad and be hard to handle. He went out a blew his whistle and some of the Village's young men came immediately. They manhandled Matthews and as soon as the handcuffs were locked he was more compliant but still cursing and swearing. Robbie and his helpers marched him to await the ferry, thinking tonight you will be safe behind bars. Robbie knew that this time Billy would go to jail because of his previous history. He would interview the lass in the morning.

Meanwhile up at the farm the girls were telling their Mum and Dad what had happened in the village with Beth Matthews. Dad was rooted to the spot while Mum full of concern asked the girls what was going to happen to Beth. As they sipped their tea they talked well into the night, not only about Beth Matthews, but also about their own family. How they could all make a fresh start.

Each of them agreed to the plan Mum had in mind to ask GanGan and Grandad to call a family meeting, with Alistair first telling his Mother the full story. Mum as usual bowed her head whilst Dad said the old bedtime prayers, which tonight seemed so alive, actually real to each of the girls and the twins. Even

Alistair caught the mood of his children and gave thanks that Him up there was listening to their pleas, and already binding them together. This certainly had never happened before. It was as if God was tangible.

Epilogue

The atmosphere in the farmhouse that evening in the Spring of '61 marked a new beginning for the McCallum Family. If you had been standing outside listening at the window you would have heard Belle playing on the piano some of the old songs they had sung as children, well they seemed old now, with the rest of family joining in the singing. There was a warmth and quiet laughter.

Madness in March was now in the past.

Printed in the United Kingdom
by Lightning Source UK Ltd.
118005UK00001B/7-54